A Rookie reader®

$22.00

Rude Ralph

Written by Justine Fontes
Illustrated by Charles Jordan

Children's Press®
A Division of Scholastic Inc.
New York • Toronto • London • Auckland • Sydney
Mexico City • New Delhi • Hong Kong
Danbury, Connecticut

EAGLE PUBLIC LIBRARY DIST.
BOX 240 EAGLE, CO 81631
(970) 328-8800

Rookie
READY TO
LEARN

Dear Parents/Educators,

Welcome to Rookie Ready to Learn. Each Rookie Reader in this series includes additional age-appropriate Let's Learn Together activity pages that help your young child to be better prepared when starting school. *Rude Ralph* offers opportunities for you and your child to talk about the important social/emotional skill of **using nice manners to make friends**. Here are early-learning skills you and your child will encounter in the *Rude Ralph* Let's Learn Together pages:

• Counting

• Vocabulary

We hope you enjoy sharing this delightful, enhanced reading experience with your early learner.

Library of Congress Cataloging-in-Publication Data

Fontes, Justine.
  Rude Ralph: rookie ready to learn/written by Justine Fontes; illustrated by Charles Jordan.
    p. cm. — (Rookie ready to learn)
  ISBN 978-0-531-26529-1 -- ISBN 978-0-531-26711-0 (pbk.)
  1. Etiquette for children and teenagers—Juvenile literature.
  2. Children--Conduct of life--Juvenile literature. 3. Friendship—Juvenile literature.
  I. Jordan, Charles. II. Title. III. Series.
  BJ1857.C5F66 2011
  395.1'22—dc22
                        2010048226

1 2 3 4 5 6 7 8 9 10 R 18 17 16 15 14 13 12 11

My friend Ralph is rude.

Ralph always cuts in line.

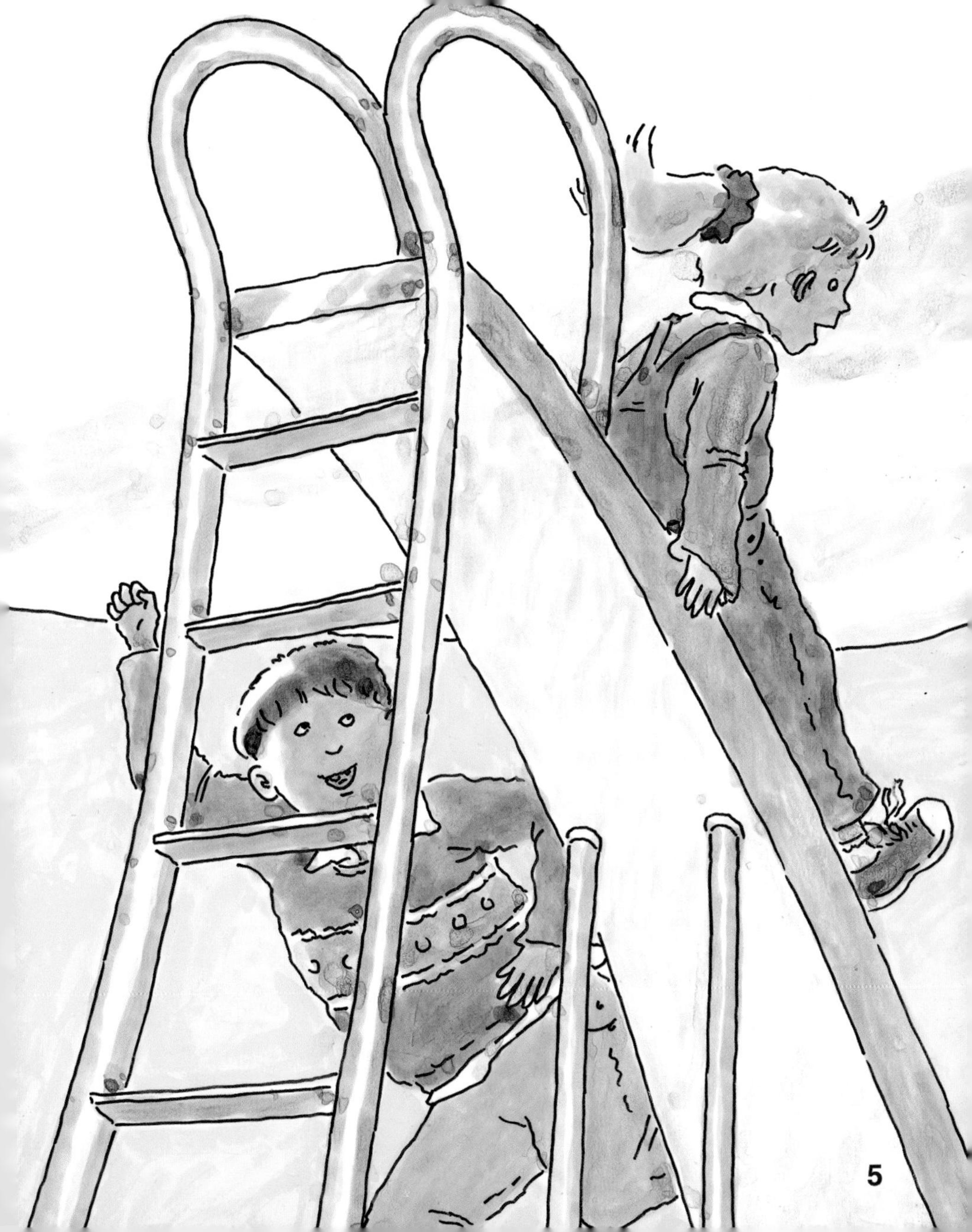

He never says, "I'm sorry."

8

He never says, "Excuse me."

Ralph never shares.

Ralph never says, "May I please?"

Tristan bumps into me.
He says "Excuse me."

Tristan lets me finish what I am saying.
He waits his turn to talk.

Tristan asks, "May I please?"
before he takes something of mine.

Tristan shares.

Tristan says, "Thank you."

Sometimes Tristan lets me go first.

25

Ralph wants to play with us.
I tell Ralph I would rather play
with someone who is polite.

27

Ralph says, "I can be polite."
I say, "Okay."

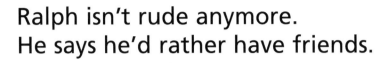

Ralph isn't rude anymore.
He says he'd rather have friends.

34

Congratulations!

You just finished reading *Rude Ralph* and learned about using your manners to be a good friend!

About the Author

Justine Fontes and her husband, Ron, hope to write 1,001 children's books — and are already more than halfway to their goal. So far they have written board books, biographies, and everything in between!

About the Illustrator

Charles Jordan lives in Pennsylvania with his wife and two children, Charlie and Maggie.

Rude Ralph

Let's learn together!

Ralph's Manners Song

(Sing this song to the tune of "Old McDonald Had a Farm.")

Ralph and I became
good friends, e, i, e, i, o.
And with my friend,
I am polite, e, i, e, i, o.
With a "thank you" here,
an "excuse me" there,
Here a "please," there a "please,"
everywhere a "please," "please."
Ralph and I became
good friends, e, i, e, i, o.

PARENT TIP: Acts of friendship can be large or small. You can help develop this important concept by being a role model and by noticing qualities of friendship you admire.

Where's Tristan?

Ralph wants to play nicely with his friends. But first he needs to find them. Use your finger to trace the path that helps Ralph find his friend.

Ralph's Favorite Things

Ralph refuses to be polite or share. He hides his toys and books. There are five toys hidden in this picture: a book, a car, a crayon, a baseball, and a bat. Can you point to them all?

The Animals Book

Being Nice

Ralph was rude until he learned how to be a good friend.

He learned to share and say "thank you." What are some other things Ralph learned that made the other children want to play with him?

▶ **PARENT TIP:** Nice manners help children make friends when playing and at school. You can help reinforce this important skill by reminding them to use their manners and telling them they did a good job when you observe them being polite, generous, considerate of others, or kind.

Be a Nice Friend

Make up a story about playing nicely with one of your friends. Say the missing word in each sentence.

I play with _____ .
_____name of someone you know_____

We play at _____ .
_____place_____

I say, "May I please play with your _____?"
_____toy_____

My friend says, "Yes. I want to share my toy with you."

I say, "Thank you."

Kindness Collage

Make a Kindness Collage with your child to celebrate the many ways friends play nicely together.

YOU WILL NEED: Old magazines Scissors

Markers Construction paper Glue stick

1 Look through the magazines and cut out pictures that show people having fun sharing, taking turns, and being kind to each other.

2 Write "Kindness Collage" at the top of a piece of paper. Glue the cutout pictures onto the poster.

Rude Ralph Word List (63 Words)

always	he	of	takes
am	he'd	okay	talk
anymore	his	play	tell
asks	I	please	thank
be	I'm	polite	to
before	in	Ralph	Tristan
bumps	into	rather	turn
can	is	rude	us
cuts	isn't	say	waits
excuse	lets	saying	wants
finish	line	says	what
first	may	shares	who
friend	me	someone	with
friends	mine	something	would
go	my	sometimes	you
have	never	sorry	

PARENT TIP: With your child, look for the polite words in the list above. Then play this polite version of Simon Says: Have your child follow the directions, but only if Simon says "please"! Call out directives such as "Simon says please put your hands on your head," and then give a directive without saying "please." Remind your child not to move if Simon doesn't say "please."